The Book of Harts Vol. 1

By Reginald Lee

Disclaimer

This book is a work of fiction. Names, characters, places, and incidents either are the product of the author's imagination or are used fictitiously. Any resemblance to actual persons, living or dead, or actual events is purely coincidental.

This novel contains adult themes, explicit language, and mature content intended for readers aged 18 and older. Reader discretion is advised.

© 2025 Reginald Lee – All Rights Reserved.

Chapter 1 – The Conversation
3

Chapter 2 – Guilty Pleasures
8

Chapter 3 – The First Date
12

Chapter 4 – Platinum Nights
18

Chapter 5 – Lost Souls
23

Chapter 6 – Secrets and Betrayal
27

Chapter 7 – The Other Man
32

Chapter 8 – Letting Go (Almost)
39

Chapter 9 – The Goodbye Letter
44

Chapter 10 – Guilty Pleasures (Again)
48

Chapter 1 – The Conversation

"It all started with a simple question: *'What's your guilty pleasure?'* For Pierre and Megan that moment marked the beginning. It was a day like any other at the office. Pierre as usual, strolled through the halls, belting out songs that stirred his soul—completely unfazed the whirlwind of activity around him. His voice echoed with carefree energy, unaware of the glances and muffled chuckles he left in his wake.

But as he neared the main office area, something —or rather, someone—caught his attention: the young woman who had recently taken over the desk by the window."

Megan sat at the desk by the window, the "new girl" who had already managed to stir more whispers in two weeks than most people did in two years. She had this calm composure about her, the kind that drew you in because you could sense there was fire beneath it. Tattoos peeking from her blouse, lip gloss just shiny enough to catch the light, and a stillness in her posture that made her seem untouchable. She didn't smile much, but her eyes? They told a different story —curiosity, challenge, maybe even invitation.

Their eyes met. Again.

They'd crossed glances before, but this time lingered. A quiet, unspoken current moved between them, charged but restrained.

Pierre broke it with a grin. "Knock knock," he said, leaning casually against her desk like he had nowhere else to be.

Megan didn't even look up from her computer screen right away. "How can I help you?" she replied, voice neutral, but her tone wasn't cold— it was… inviting, like she already knew he wasn't here for business.

Pierre skipped small talk and went straight for the deep end, firing off questions with that reckless confidence that came so naturally to him.

"Do you believe someone can love two people?" he asked.

Megan finally looked up, surprised by the question but not thrown off. "Depends," she said simply.

Pierre smirked and kept going. "Is unconditional love really unconditional?"

Her lips curved just slightly, like she was amused by the challenge. "Only if you're ready to test it."

Pierre tilted his head, enjoying her sharpness. "At what age is too old to stop saying *that's my boyfriend* or *that's my girlfriend*?"

Megan leaned back in her chair, arms folded now. She answered him effortlessly, like she'd been waiting on someone to throw her these kinds of questions. Each response was quick, playful, and intelligent. She didn't let his charisma rattle her. If anything, she leaned into it.

Inside, Megan was biting back a smile. *This is mental foreplay,* she thought. *And damn if that isn't a turn-on.*

Pierre's grin widened as he caught the flicker in her expression. He could tell she was playing along, but not pretending. This wasn't the usual office flirt. This was sharper. Deeper. And a hell of a lot more dangerous.

Their conversation drifted past office noise, past time, past rules. Every word was a small dare. Every answer was another thread pulling them closer together.

Pierre leaned down just slightly, lowering his voice. "You know, there are—or soon will be—rumors about us. These people don't have a life of their own. Should I stop coming by your office?"

Megan didn't hesitate. She looked him dead in the eye. "No. Let them talk."

The air shifted then. Neither of them moved, but the weight of their chemistry filled the space.

Around them, coworkers typed and whispered, but in that moment it felt like the room belonged only to them.

That's when Pierre dropped the line—half slick, half serious. "Take my number. Call me when you're sure."

It was something he'd stolen from a rap lyric, but it landed.

Megan's lips parted, then curved into a sly smile. Without breaking eye contact, she typed something into her phone. A second later, Pierre's pocket buzzed.

He pulled out his phone, and there it was: a text from her.

"You can call now."

Pierre couldn't stop the laugh that slipped out of him. Smooth. She had just flipped his own line back on him, putting the ball squarely in his court.

And just like that, the game had begun.

Chapter 2 – Guilty Pleasures

Their eyes kept finding each other after that first exchange. Passing glances in the hallway, subtle smiles during meetings, the kind of energy that coworkers noticed even when neither of them said a word.

Pierre told himself it was harmless. Just a little fun, a little flirt. Megan? She was careful not to give away too much. Still, the office buzz had shifted. People whispered. Some chuckled, others raised brows. And Pierre, bold as always, didn't bother hiding it.

One late afternoon, he leaned against Megan's desk again.

"What's your guilty pleasure?" he asked suddenly, his tone casual but his eyes sharp.

Megan tilted her head, like she'd been waiting for him to cross this line. The question wasn't really about guilty pleasures—it was about how much of herself she was willing to let him see.

She tapped her pen against the desk, pretending to think. Then she smiled — slow, deliberate. "I love spending weekends on my couch naked… just eating and watching movies."

Pierre's eyebrows lifted, his smirk widening as he let the words hang between them. The image came alive in his head, vivid and unfiltered.

Megan leaned in, her voice lowering. "How about you, Pierre?"

He chuckled, shaking his head. "I like dipping cookies in milk… also without clothes on."

Megan's laugh was soft but real, the kind that slipped past her defenses. She grinned, clearly intrigued.

Pierre studied her, then did something that caught her off guard. He reached across the desk and took her hand. The touch was deliberate, not rushed.

Her breath hitched. She hadn't expected it, but she didn't pull away either. His palm was warm, his grip firm but not demanding.

"See how perfectly your hand fits in mine?" he said, eyes searching hers.

Something flickered in Megan's chest. Dangerous. Intoxicating.

A pause stretched out between them, heavy but sweet.

Her words came out steady, but inside she felt the thrum of adrenaline. She hadn't meant for this to happen, but there was something about Pierre she couldn't ignore. The way he carried himself—older, grounded, but playful. It wasn't just attraction; it was curiosity.

From then on, the magnetic pull between them only grew harder to hide.

In meetings, she caught herself sneaking glances at him, watching the way his lips moved when he spoke, the way his laughter filled a room. At lunch, they'd pass each other in the hallway, exchanging looks that meant more than words ever could. Even the most innocent conversations felt charged.

And people noticed. They always do. Whispers followed them like shadows. Eyes lingered a little too long. Some coworkers smirked knowingly; others looked uncomfortable.

But Pierre and Megan? They didn't care.

It was too late to stop the spark that had already caught fire.

Chapter 3 – The First Date

The more Pierre tried to keep his distance, the more his thoughts drifted back to Megan. Her sharp answers replayed in his head, the way her laugh slipped out like she was trying to hide it but couldn't, the way her hand fit in his. He told himself he wasn't pressed—*he was grown, he'd seen plenty of women come and go*—but there was something different about this one.

One night, scrolling through his phone and fighting the urge to text her, Pierre leaned into boldness instead. He snapped a picture of the tequila bottle sitting on his counter and slid into her messages.

Come have a drink with your boy, he typed.

It was simple, straight to the point, his way of saying *I want you here* without saying too much.

Her reply came quick.
Not tonight, Megan wrote, a little playful. *I've got plans with my girls.*

Pierre smirked, shaking his head. He wasn't surprised. She seemed like the type who always had somewhere to be, people to see, nights that weren't meant for him. Still, he couldn't deny the sting of disappointment.

So he grabbed the bottle, stepped outside, and sure enough, his neighbor John was posted up like always—drink in one hand, smoke in the other, the night stretching out easy around him.

"What's up, OG?" John grinned when he saw Pierre. "Let's have a drink."

Pierre passed him the bottle, settling in beside him. They clinked the glasses together before taking shots, the bite of the liquor burning warm in their throats.

As the night air cooled around them, Pierre found himself talking. He told John about Megan—this young woman at his job who had him all the way twisted. He bragged on her beauty, her tattoos, her intelligence. How she didn't just laugh at his jokes but threw fire back at him, matching his energy question for question, thought for thought.

"She got a mind that turns me on, man," Pierre admitted, his voice low but lit with something real. "She's younger, yeah... but different."

John let out a laugh, taking another pull from the bottle. "Sounds like a vibe. Go for it, OG. What you waiting on?"

Pierre thought about that for a second. *What was he waiting on?* He wasn't the type to hesitate, but with Megan, he found himself overthinking. Maybe it was the age gap. Maybe it was how slick she was. Maybe it was because, for the first time in a long time, he felt like he had something to lose.

But John's words stuck. *Go for it*.

So he did.

The next day, Pierre asked Megan out for Saturday. He braced himself for excuses, but instead she fired back quick:

"Let's go bowling. I bet I can beat you!"

Pierre smiled at the text, shaking his head. She had no idea. He wasn't about to let her win without a fight.

All week, anticipation built. Their texts turned playful, more flirt than small talk. By the time Saturday rolled around, Pierre could feel it in his chest—the sense that this night was going to change something.

When Megan stepped out of her apartment, Pierre froze. Damn. She was stunning. Jeans that hugged her just right, a top that showed off her ink, her hair framing her face like she knew exactly what she was doing.

"Damn," he muttered under his breath before pulling it together and striding to open her door like a gentleman.

"You need a step stool or you good?" he teased as she climbed in.

Megan shot him a *boy, please* look, trying not to laugh. The spark was already there, crackling between them.

The drive to the bowling alley was filled with playful digs, subtle compliments, and stretches of silence that didn't feel awkward at all. Pierre liked the way Megan talked—confident, sharp, but sweet underneath. Megan liked the way he carried himself—laid-back but intentional, that quiet grown-man confidence that didn't need to prove anything.

When they stepped into the bowling alley, they didn't even hesitate. Straight to the bar. Two shots. Then another. By the time they hit the lanes, they were both buzzing, loose and ready.

Pierre locked in immediately, focused and competitive. Megan? Not so much. Her first throw wobbled down the gutter.

"The only reason you're winning is because I hurt my hand the other day," she said, half-pouting, half-laughing.

Pierre raised a brow. "Oh, so that's the excuse?"

She playfully shoved him, then lined up for another throw—this time hitting only two pins. Pierre shook his head, fighting back a grin.

The game wrapped, the shots hit, and the night spilled outside. North Hills was electric—cars thumping music, people spilling out of restaurants, voices rising in the air. But for Pierre and Megan, it all blurred into background noise.

"What's next?" Pierre asked, his eyes locked on hers.

She held his gaze, a slow smile tugging at her lips.

"Take me to your place," she said softly.

Pierre didn't need to hear it twice.

Chapter 4 – Platinum Nights

The drive back to Pierre's place felt like it took both forever and no time at all. The city lights blurred past, neon streaks against the glass, but Pierre barely noticed. His hands were tight on the steering wheel, knuckles flexing as if they were holding back more than just the car.

Megan leaned over in her seat, reapplying lip gloss slowly, deliberately, each swipe catching the light from the passing street lamps. When Pierre glanced at her, she was already watching him. Her smile curved, sly and knowing.

Halfway down the highway, she reached over and tugged at the knot of his drawstring.

Pierre's eyes flicked down, then back to the road. "You wild," he muttered, but he didn't stop her.

Her fingers slipped beneath the fabric, and when her hand closed around him, her eyes widened.

"Damn," Megan whispered, unable to keep it to herself. "You're large."

Pierre chuckled, trying to keep his focus on the road, but the warmth of her touch had his foot pressing heavier on the gas. The car swerved just slightly before he corrected it, gripping the wheel like his life depended on it.

"Girl, you gon' make me wreck this damn car," he said through gritted teeth.

Megan just smirked and leaned in further. Within seconds, her lips replaced her hand, her head moving in rhythm as Pierre's body tensed and relaxed all at once.

His breath grew uneven, his chest rising and falling like he'd just run a sprint. The twenty-minute ride shrank to ten, Pierre's pulse matching the beat of the tires on the road. By the time he pulled into his driveway, he was already halfway undone.

They barely made it through the door. Shoes kicked off, jackets sliding to the floor, lips colliding in a rush that was both hungry and hesitant—hungry for the moment, hesitant only in that they knew this was no turning back.

Pierre pressed her against the hallway wall, tracing the curve of her tattoos with his fingertips, committing each line of ink to memory.

"There is no greater feeling," he murmured, "than sliding down the panties of new pussy."

Megan laughed breathlessly, tugging at his shirt until it joined the pile on the floor. Her skin was warm, soft, glowing beneath the dim light of his living room lamp.

By the time they reached the bedroom, Pierre was already fumbling for a condom.

When he slid into her, the air shifted. Megan's eyes widened, her body arching as a sharp cry escaped her lips.

Pierre grinned, that lyric echoing in his head. *She fucked up when she gave me some pussy.*

Every stroke deepened the rhythm, every shift of position pulling new sounds from her, until words blurred into moans and gasps. Megan's nails raked down his back, her voice breaking as she whispered the number—seven.

Pierre laughed breathlessly. "How many nuts is that?"

"Seven," she panted, her body trembling beneath his.

Morning light crept in through the blinds, golden streaks falling across tangled sheets. They lay there for a while, breathing in sync, their bodies exhausted but unwilling to separate just yet.

Megan turned to him, her lips curling into a soft smile. "I thought you were a square," she teased. "But you're the real deal. Must be that Fayetteville swag you talk about."

Pierre laughed, brushing his thumb across her cheek. In that quiet moment, something shifted—something deeper than lust, something that whispered *this ain't just one night*.

He asked the question softly, almost like he was afraid of the answer. "Am I the only one you're sleeping with?"

"Yes," Megan replied, steady and sure. "And you will be the only one."

"So no condoms?" he pressed.

"No."

Pierre nodded, letting out a slow breath. "Promise me something, then. If you ever sleep with someone else, tell me. I don't like to share. Even as a kid, I never shared my toys. I just want the choice to decide whether to keep this going."

Megan looked at him, her face serious now. "I promise."

Pierre smiled faintly, pulling her close again. In his mind, the promise was enough. In his heart, though, he didn't realize just how heavy those words would one day become.

For now, he let himself believe.

Chapter 5 – Lost Souls

What followed was a whirlwind—part lust, part hunger, part something neither of them wanted to name.

They couldn't keep their hands off each other. Every brush of skin, every stolen glance felt like a dare, and neither of them had the will to resist. What started as subtle touches at her desk soon spilled over into risky territory.

At work, they stole moments like thieves. Pierre would lean into Megan's office, door cracked just enough to keep up appearances. The blinds never fully closed, and maybe that was part of the thrill. He'd bend her over the desk, her hand clutching at papers she pretended to organize, while Pierre whispered filth in her ear, low enough to be drowned out by the hum of the copy machine down the hall.

Some days, it was the backseat of his car during lunch breaks. The tinted windows fogged up fast, the air thick with the mix of sweat, perfume, and the sound of her muffled laughter when he said something slick between kisses.

Other days, it was Pierre's couch, neither of them able to wait until nightfall. Megan's shoes left in the entryway, her blouse tossed over the armrest, Pierre grinning as if every time was his first time.

But it wasn't just the sex.

That's what caught Pierre off guard.

Because when the sweat dried and their clothes were back on, the conversations flowed like another kind of intimacy. They talked for hours, sometimes about nothing, sometimes about everything. Dreams, childhood memories, things they'd never told another soul.

Megan would sit cross-legged on the couch, her hair falling across her face, listening intently as Pierre told stories from his past—about the Ville, about mistakes he'd made, about the nights he almost gave up and the mornings he somehow pushed through.

"You know," she said one night, looking at him with a mix of curiosity and softness, "I thought you were just another old head trying to chase young women. But you... you're more than that."

Pierre laughed, shaking his head. "Don't gas me up. I just like good conversation."

Megan smirked. "Conversation, huh? That what you call it?"

Still, Pierre couldn't shake the thought. She was young, beautiful, intelligent, successful. He couldn't figure out why someone like her would want to give him this much of her time.

The nights blurred into mornings. The mornings turned into weeks. And the promise she'd given him —*you're the only one*—echoed in his mind like both a comfort and a warning.

Pierre wanted to believe her.

But something in him knew better.

Every time she pulled away after work, every weekend she spent with her girlfriends instead of him, the doubts crept in. He told himself to ignore them, to just enjoy the ride, but the more he fell into her world, the harder it was to protect his own heart.

Still, he couldn't stop. He didn't *want* to stop.

For Pierre, Megan wasn't just a woman—she was a storm, pulling him deeper with every kiss, every conversation, every promise she wasn't sure she could keep.

And Pierre? He was already lost in it.

Chapter 6 – Secrets and Betrayal

The new year came in quietly. Fireworks popped in the distance, glasses clinked, and resolutions filled the air—but none of that mattered much to Pierre. He was exactly where he wanted to be: Megan on his couch, her feet tucked under his thigh, her laughter spilling out as they played dominoes late into the night.

They had started a tradition—drinks, games, and long talks. Megan sipped tequila like it was water, her cheeks warm, her voice looser with each pour. Pierre didn't drink much, but tonight he let himself match her shot for shot.

The vibe was easy. Comfortable. Too comfortable.

Because when Megan's phone buzzed on the cushion beside her, she picked it up without hesitation, unlocked it, and handed it to him to look at a meme she'd been laughing at earlier.

Pierre wasn't snooping. Not at first. But as his eyes flicked across the screen, something caught him—a name, a message, a line that didn't belong.

Then another.

And another.

The tequila haze cleared instantly.

He scrolled, slow at first, then faster, his pulse hammering in his ears. The words stared back at him, undeniable: Megan had been sleeping with two other men for months.

The bottle in his hand suddenly felt heavy, his throat dry, his stomach hot with anger.

At 3 a.m., he ripped the covers off her. "Get your ass outta my bed," he snapped, his voice sharp enough to cut the air.

Megan stirred, half-asleep, confused. "What? What's wrong?"

"You've been lying," Pierre said, holding up her phone like evidence. "Sleeping with other people this whole time."

Megan sat up, her face pale now despite the alcohol still in her system. She hadn't realized she'd given him access, hadn't thought about what he might find.

"Pierre, wait—" she started, reaching for him.

But he stepped back, jaw clenched, eyes burning. The trust he thought they had was unraveling in real time.

Megan pulled her clothes on quickly, fumbling with her shoes as the reality sank in. Then she was gone, the door slamming shut behind her.

The house felt too quiet. Too empty. Pierre sat on the edge of the bed, her phone still in his hand, his chest aching. He wanted to scream, to throw the phone against the wall, to erase every word he'd just read.

Instead, he stared at the blank space she'd left behind.

Minutes turned into hours.

Then his phone buzzed.

Megan: *I tried to cut them off, but things got complicated. I only want you. I swear I'll block them and end everything if you don't leave me.*

Pierre read the message over and over. His anger fought against the part of him that still wanted her. *Why does she get this much control over me?* he thought.

He knew he wasn't innocent himself. He'd been with other women—empty nights, no feelings, just bodies. But this was different. This was betrayal dressed as love.

And yet, when she texted again—apologies spilling across the screen, promises to change, pleas for another chance—Pierre's resolve softened.

He told himself they weren't official and that everyone makes mistakes. He told himself the chemistry was too strong to walk away, so he forgave her.

Not fully. Not truly. But enough to let her back in.

Though Pierre let her return to his bed, the trust between them had been fractured. And once a crack shows, no matter how small, it only spreads.

Chapter 7 – The Other Man

For a while, things seemed patched together. Pierre told himself he'd forgiven Megan, that they could start fresh. They were official now, and he wanted to believe that meant something.

But the cracks were there. Always there.

During the week, she was all his—texting nonstop, falling asleep in his arms, laughing at his jokes, letting him rub her feet after long days. But the weekends? The weekends were different.

Friday would come, and she'd say she had plans with her girls. Saturday, she'd vanish until the afternoon. Sunday, her texts slowed to a trickle. Pierre tried to play it cool, tried to remind himself that she was young, that she had a life outside of him. But inside, he felt the absence like an open wound.

"Time is the only thing we can't get back," he'd told her once, his voice heavy.

Megan had laughed softly, kissing his cheek. "Relax. I'm young. I have plenty of time."

Pierre nodded, but her words stuck like a thorn.

He started protecting himself. He told himself it wasn't wrong to see other women on the side, especially since Megan's loyalty was shaky. Jess was the main one—sweet, easy, no drama. They'd been seeing each other for a couple months, and while Jess didn't set his soul on fire the way Megan did, she filled the void when Megan disappeared.

Still, Megan lingered at the center of his world.

One Saturday morning, after leaving Jess's place, Pierre decided to swing by Megan's apartment. He called. No answer. He texted. Nothing.

As he pulled into the lot, his chest tightened. The door opened. And there she was—Megan—stepping outside with another man.

Pierre's stomach dropped.

The man was tall, lean, his presence casual but telling. He and Megan side-hugged at the door like it wasn't their first time. Later, Pierre would learn his name: Chase.

Pierre's car slowed as he pulled in behind hers. His grip on the steering wheel turned white.

Megan's eyes widened the second she spotted him. She froze, then rushed to her car, fumbling with her keys.

"I have to go to work!" she blurted, sliding inside. Before Pierre could even open his mouth, she backed out and drove off fast, leaving him sitting there, heat rising in his chest.

The rest of the day was silence. No call. No explanation.

Then his phone rang that night.

"That was just a friend from work," Megan said quickly, her voice rushed, shaky. "His girlfriend kicked him out, and he needed a place to crash. He slept on the couch."

Pierre's voice was low, steady, dangerous. "So… nothing happened?"

"No!" she insisted. "I don't deserve you, Pierre. You're a great guy and I love you. But I don't know how to love. Teach me how to love! I swear to you, I'm not lying… nothing happened."

Her words hit him in two places at once—soft and sharp. Part of him wanted to believe her. Part of him already knew better.

Every day after that, Pierre doubled down on showing her love. He sent her romantic quotes, rubbed her back when it hurt, massaged her feet when she was tired. He gave and gave, even when something in his gut told him she wasn't giving the same in return.

But weekends still slipped away. Mother's Day weekend—no Megan. Memorial Day—still gone. Excuses piled up like bricks between them.

Then came the night that broke it.

Pierre was visiting a friend when he saw a familiar car pull up to a house down the street. His chest tightened. Megan.

She had told him she was going to her brother's party in Durham. But this wasn't Durham. And the house she walked into? Belonged to Chase.

Pierre's feet moved before his mind caught up. He walked up the path and rang the doorbell.

The door opened.

Chase.

"Is Megan here?" Pierre asked, his voice clipped.

Chase squinted, sizing him up. "Who are you?"

"I'm her brother," Pierre lied quickly.

Chase hesitated. "Hold on." He disappeared inside.

Pierre paced on the porch, adrenaline rushing, thoughts spinning. *What if she's in there with him right now? What if she's lying in his bed?* His chest felt like it might explode.

Moments later, Chase returned alone. His face was colder now. "She doesn't want to come out. Who are you?"

Pierre's jaw tightened. "I'm her man. Well… I was her man."

The words came out like broken glass.

Later that night, his phone rang.

"You followed me?" Megan's voice snapped through the line. "Meet me at the gas station."

Pierre's heart pounded as he pulled into the bright glow of the pumps. She was there, waiting, her face tense but unreadable.

"It's over," she said flatly.

The silence that followed was heavier than any argument. Pierre stared at her, searching for something—remorse, regret, anything.

"Why did you keep me around then?" His voice cracked, sharp with pain. "All those times I tried to leave… why didn't you let me go?"

Megan looked away. "I don't know."

Pierre let out a bitter laugh, the kind that carried more pain than humor. "Two years of my life. Wasted. Does he fuck better?"

"No."

"Am I too old?"

"No."

"Then what in the fuck is it?" he demanded.

"I don't know!" she cried, her voice breaking.

Pierre stepped back, his chest hollow. "Don't call me anymore. We're done."

"Okay," she whispered, almost too softly.

And just like that, the music inside him stopped.

There were no more songs to sing.

Chapter 8 – Letting Go (Almost)

The silence after the gas station felt like punishment.

Pierre had told her not to call, not to text. He'd meant it. At least, he thought he did. His house was too quiet without her laughter, his bed too cold without her body pressed against his. Every song on the radio seemed to carry her voice.

Days crawled.

No missed calls.
No texts.
Nothing.

And then, just when his chest had started to harden, her name lit up his screen.

I miss you.

Pierre stared at the message, his thumb hovering. He knew better. He knew exactly what this was —her way of keeping the door cracked just enough to walk back in whenever she pleased. And yet, his chest loosened at the sight of it.

Before long, they were meeting again. First it was dinner, then drinks.

"Do you want to have sex?" she asked bluntly, like she was asking for a glass of water.

Without missing a beat, Pierre answered, "Yes. Wear nothing but a robe. I have a fantasy football draft later… I'll be there in ten minutes."

Megan laughed softly, feeling her juices rush down her leg. "In your car?"

"Yeah!"

Pierre pulled up naked in front of her complex.

"Out here?" she asked. "My neighbors will see!"

"It's nothing but ass and titties, pussy and dick."

Megan immediately sucking on Pierre's nipples, while using the wetness from her vagina to caress his dick. She alternated between licking his nipples and sucking his dick. She knew Pierre well. "You want me huh?" Wrapping her lips around the thickness of his **Y vein.** "Your shit is extra swollen!"

Fighting back the nut, Pierre responded. "What took you so long?"

Reaching her boiling point, she slid Pierre inside, instantly cummn! Eyes rolled to the back, shaking, they could hear the dick and pussy collision.

Pierre could see the cum on his **Y vein** and feel it against his scrotum as Megan rode up and down.

It didn't help that Pierre began to choke her while pulling her hair simultaneously. Pierre didn't know if he was choking her because it was in the moment or because of his frustration with her.

Either way, Pierre was tearing that ass up! "You going to give that pussy tomorrow?"

"Hell fuck yeah!"

"Fuck Pierre, fuck!"

For the next three days, Megan and Pierre had great, erotic, spontaneous sex.

But when Friday rolled around, Megan disappeared again.

Weekends weren't his. They belonged to Chase.

Pierre knew it. He even drove past Chase's house sometimes, hoping not to see her car in the driveway. But there it was, always there, parked like it belonged. Each time, the sight of it ripped another piece of him away.

"I hate that bitch," he muttered to himself one night, gripping the steering wheel so tight his knuckles whitened. "Fuck her. She trying to have her cake and eat it too. I'm moving on."

But the truth was written across his face in the rearview mirror.

He still loved her.

No matter how many times he cursed her name, no matter how many other women he slept with trying to fill the void, it was Megan who lived in his chest.

And she knew it.

Chapter 9 – The Goodbye Letter

Pierre had always been better with words than with silence. Silence left too much room for his thoughts to chase themselves in circles. So when he finally decided he was done, really done, he reached for a pen instead of his phone.

The paper sat blank for a long time. He stared at it, the tip of the pen hovering, his hand heavy. What do you even write to a woman who's broken you but still has pieces of your soul in her pocket?

He started simple.

Megan,

The ink bled into the page, steady but slow.

I don't have the energy to argue with you anymore. I've said all I could say. I've given you more chances than you ever deserved. And yet, every time I told myself to leave, you pulled me back in. And every time, I let you.

He paused, took a breath, then kept going.

I've rubbed your feet when they hurt. I've held you when you were tired. I've listened to your dreams and your fears. I've given you every piece of love I knew how to give. And you gave me lies in return.

The pen scratched harder against the paper now, his frustration leaking through.

I'm selfish. I told you that from the start. I never liked sharing, not even when I was a kid. I don't like sharing my toys, and I damn sure don't like sharing my woman. And yet, here I am, competing with a man who shouldn't even be in your life. That ain't love. That's torture.

His chest tightened. He swallowed hard, blinked, and forced his hand to steady.

So here it is, plain and simple: I'm done. This is goodbye. Don't call me. Don't text me. Don't show up. Because if you do, I know myself—I'll fold. And I can't keep folding for you.

He set the pen down, staring at the words as if they might rearrange themselves into something softer. But they didn't. They stayed raw, sharp, final.

Folding the letter neatly, he slid it into an envelope and left it on her dresser the next time he saw her. He didn't explain. Didn't add more than what was already written.

No more arguments.
No more questions.
No more words.

For the first time in months, Pierre felt a strange kind of calm. Not peace exactly—because peace would mean he'd stopped loving her, and he hadn't—but calm in the way that comes when you've finally decided to put your pain down instead of carrying it.

Megan didn't say much when she found the letter. She read it quietly, her expression unreadable, then tucked it away somewhere Pierre couldn't see.

And that was it.

Another week passed.

The silence returned.

But this time, it wasn't a punishment. It was the end of something that had been dying all along.

Chapter 10 – Guilty Pleasures (Again)

The silence stretched on longer this time.

Pierre didn't check his phone the way he used to. He didn't wait for her name to flash across the screen. He told himself the letter was the end —that he'd finally done what he should have done months ago. He'd shed enough tears over the years. Love is tricky.

And in some ways, it was true. The house was still quiet, but it didn't ache the same way anymore. The music he used to hum to himself came back, little by little. He even started laughing again—not the bitter kind, but the real kind, the kind that caught him off guard.

But nights were still the hardest. Nights had a way of reminding him that even though he'd let her go, pieces of her still lingered. The smell of her lotion on the pillow. The faint mark of her lipstick on one of his glasses. Ghosts in the spaces she used to fill.

One evening, as Pierre was winding down, his phone lit up with an unfamiliar number. For a moment, he thought about ignoring it. But something made him answer.

"Hello?"

There was a pause on the other end. A voice he didn't recognize, low and hesitant.

"Can we talk?"

Pierre frowned. "Who is this?"

"It's Chase," the voice said. "I'm... I'm confused, man. I got questions."

Made in the USA
Middletown, DE
18 October 2025